Look at Me

Charlotte Hall Ricks

Illustrated by Annie Gusman

HOUGHTON MIFFLIN COMPANY BOSTON 1979

Library of Congress Cataloging in Publication Data

Ricks, Charlotte Hall
  Look at me.

  SUMMARY: Mother is too busy to pay attention to
Catherine's antics until Catherine, in exasperation,
carries out her threat to disappear.
  [1.   Mother and child – Fiction]   I.   Gusman, Annie.
II.   Title.
PZ7.R41615Lo   [E]   79-14463

ISBN 0-395-28480-5

H   10   9   8   7   6   5   4   3   2   1

Look at Me

"Play with me?" said Catherine. "Read to me?"

"Not now," said Mother.

"Look at me," said Catherine. "I'm a monkey."

"I can't look now," said Mother. "I'm busy."

"Look at me," said Catherine. "I can do cartwheels. I can do
twenty cartwheels all around the living room."

"Very good," said Mother. "But watch out for the coffee table."

"I'm swimming," said Catherine. "I can swim under the water and on top of the water."

"Fine," said Mother. "But don't splash on the floor."

"Look at me," said Catherine. "I can eat one hundred cookies."

"Don't spoil your appetite," said Mother.

"I can sing. I can sing the whole 'Blue-Tail Fly,'" said
Catherine.

"Not too loud," said Mother. "You'll wake the baby."

"I can play the piano with both hands," said Catherine.
"I can play the Chopin Waltz in C# Minor."

"Lovely," said Mother. "But wash your hands first."

"Look at me. I'm flying," said Catherine.

"Fine," said Mother.

"I can fly," said Catherine. "I can fly out one window and in the other."

"Lovely," said Mother. "But don't go out without your sweater." 21

"I can disappear. I can really disappear," said Catherine.

"What?" said Mother. But Catherine had already gone.

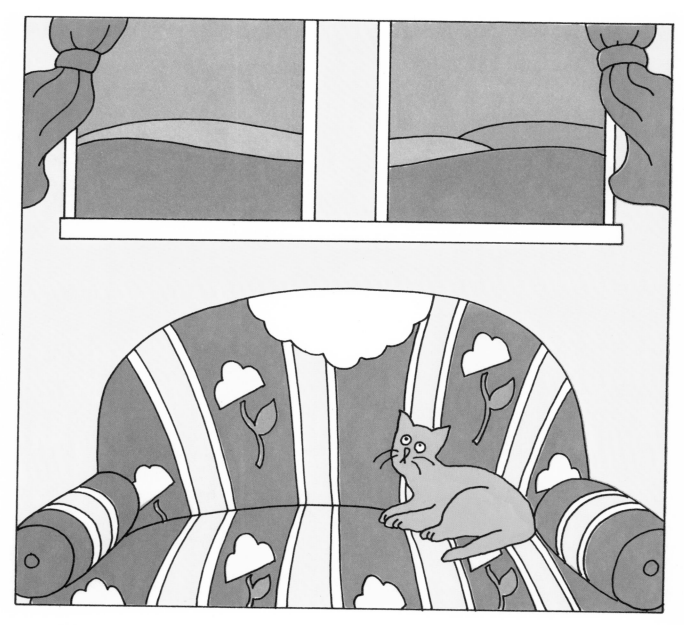

"Catherine!" said Mother.

"CATHERINE!"

"CATHERINE!"

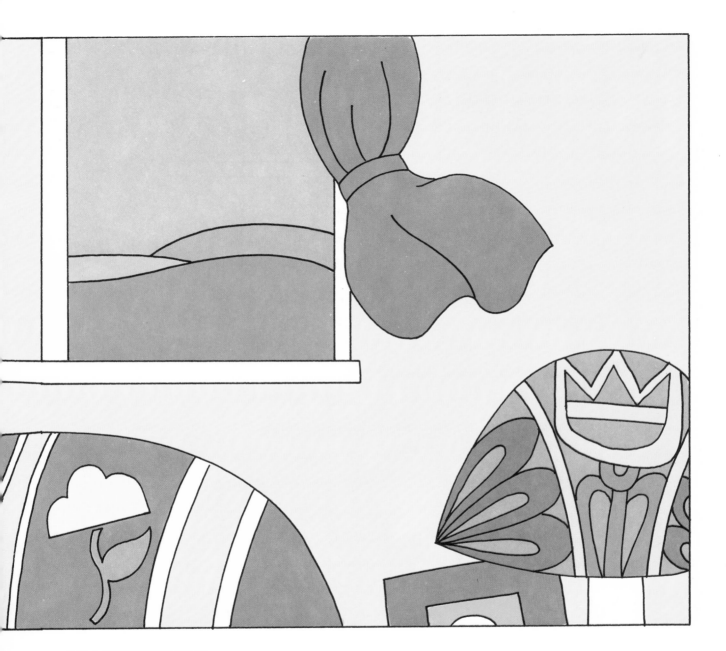

"CATHERINE!"

"I won't come back until you promise me nine hundred and
ninety-nine kisses," said Catherine.

"I can't see you. Come back, come back," said Mother.

"Here I am," said Catherine.

"There you are," said Mother. "I missed you."

"And here's a THOUSAND kisses," said Mother.